THE REWARD

THE REWARD

by

Kenneth Fly

Gotham Books

30 N Gould St.
Ste. 20820, Sheridan, WY 82801
https://gothambooksinc.com/

Phone: 1 (307) 464-7800

© 2025 *Kenneth Fly*. All rights reserved.

No part of this book may be reproduced, stored in a retrieval system, or transmitted by any means without the written permission of the author.

Published by Gotham Books (May 10, 2025)

ISBN: 979-8-3492-4044-7 (P)
ISBN: 979-8-3492-4045-4 (E)

Because of the dynamic nature of the Internet, any web addresses or links contained in this book may have changed since publication and may no longer be valid.

The views expressed in this work are solely those of the author and do not necessarily reflect the views of the publisher, and the publisher hereby disclaims any responsibility for them.

TABLE OF CONTENTS

FORWARD vi
CHAPTER 1 1
CHAPTER 2 2
CHAPTER 3 3
CHAPTER 4 4
CHAPTER 5 7
CHAPTER 6 10
CHAPTER 7 13
CHAPTER 8 15
CHAPTER 9 16
CHAPTER 10 17
CHAPTER 11 21
CHAPTER 12 23
CHAPTER 13 27
CHAPTER 14 30
CHAPTER 15 31
CHAPTER 16 32
CHARACTERS 37
GALLERY 38

FORWARD

The setting is in the early 1880's where a man and a woman settled in the beautiful slopes near the Arizona mountains with the dream of building their future on homestead property as a rancher and a family of several children. This is the story of the hard life with many disappointments, including the way ward son and his disturbed life.

CHAPTER 1

Jed and Molly Rime arrived in their land of dreams near the mountain on a beautiful slope rich with good farm dirt and a never-ending source of water. Living in the covered wagon on which they had made the long journey they began to gather the necessary stones and logs needed to build their new log cabin.

Jed and Molly worked feverishly to finish enough shelter before the winter set in. The time passed and their health was good through the fall season reaching their goal of the one room cabin. Because of their early planning they had brought along a cow and of course they had the horses that had delivered them by wagon to their new land of dreams.

The summer and fall were a daylight to dark job for them both. The determination to survive resulted in a productive crop and garden. Now that winter was to set in Jed and Molly began to realize that winter was not going to be easy protecting themselves, the horses, cow and fowls they had purchased by helping other settlers was sometimes an all-night job.

CHAPTER 2

Winter had hardly gotten underway when the news of Molly's expecting their first child was sooner than expected but now the family had begun. The happiness they felt from the news was hampered by the concern of not being ready for a baby. The winter passed slowly and the weather had been fierce that year but with spring right around the corner they planned all the necessary moves that had to be made in order to progress and build on their new life.

Molly progressing quickly with her pregnancy but was strong and was able to do most all the work necessary for the crops they had planned. She did all the milking, cooking, and garden work while Jed was busy hunting, building the barn and necessary fencing to house the animals.

CHAPTER 3

Spring brought the blessing of a healthy boy who was given the name Billy in honor of his grandfather, who was Jed's father that was not healthy enough to make the journey west and had now passed away.

Billy was a healthy baby and Jed had great hopes of building a successful ranch to pass on to Billy and hopefully other future children.

The children came quickly to Jed a Molly without any complications. As time passed Jed and Molly were determined to have several children and did so. Within an eight year period a total of six children was born to Jed and Molly, two boys and four girls. The oldest of course was Billy, being the oldest boy child he was expected to do a goodly amount of the work and taking care of the younger siblings while Jed and Molly kept everything going on the farm.

As a young boy Billy seemed to become bitter and have a mean streak developing. A rebelling attitude toward his father Jed. Now this was not the picture Jed had in his mind and did not fit his plan to have a happy family. In turn the pressure effected both their attitude and in turn spread though the whole family. At an early age Billy tried to figure out how to get away from this messed up family, but never could get the courage to leave.

CHAPTER 4

Finally at age twelve Billy decided to take one of the horses and ride into town being about a five mile ride and doing so he left all his required chores behind to be done by Jed an d other younger members of the family.

While in town Billy entered the saloon and talked the bar man into giving him a taste of some rotgut whiskey. He downed the shot without a reaction just like a man to the amazement of the rough and rowdy guys pushing his hand to see if he could do it again. Sure enough the second shot went down just as easy. As you might have guessed this was the first start of a long road of wild and lawless life.

This event resulted in the sheriff interning the saloon, running everyone out, collaring the young man and taking him home. Jed had put up with about all he could and the beating he gave Billy was the worst yet. With a warning from the sheriff to Jed and Billy he went on his way back to town.

That night was a true turning point for the young Billy and when everyone was asleep he took the best saddle horse, filled a sack with a few supplies a n d his dads six gun and lit out across the country. He didn't know where he was headed but anywhere to get away from the hard life and brutal beatings.

He rode all night in order to put as much distance between him and his past life as he passably could. Unaware of the dangers he would face, he found himself surrounded by a gang of outlaws who took his mount leaving him all alone far from home, so what was he to do now but to figure out how to survive the best way he could on his own. As luck would have it they did not take his bag of supplies where he had hidden the six shooter he had taken from his Dad.

After a little rest Billy decided to find a homestead family and find a place to stay for a spell and work to make enough to move on. Shortly he came upon a homestead (small ranch) and presented himself as an orphan whose parents had been killed in a raid. Feeling sorry for the young boy the farmer took him in and found he was a good hand and was able to do most anything that needed to be done around the place.

Some time had passed and the couple grew fond of the boy as they had no children of their own and treated him as one of the family. At the dinner table one evening after a hard day of fence building the conversation turned to family and the rancher's wife asked for some details of Billy's past. For some reason at a weak moment he told of his boyhood and about the way he was treated, even taking part of the blame for doing some of the things he had done and revealed the fact that he had run away from home without any plans for the future.

In disbelief, after hearing the original story of his parents being killed in a raid, the man asked

"Where is this farm your family settled on and how big a family he came from".

Billy told them that he had a brother and four sisters younger than he and at times wondered how they were fairing, wondering if the brothers and sister was going through the same thing he had to endure.

"I know about where your homestead is and really it is not too far from here. You must have traveled in a circle before coming up on our place".

"What do you think of going back home and giving it another try".

Billy was not too keen on the idea of having to face his dad but would like very much to see his mother, brother and sisters. After he slept on the idea he decided to go back home just to see how things were.

Being a kind hear ted person and having developed a liking for the boy the rancher said I will go back with you and maybe that would make it easier. So off went across the country in the direction of the homestead.

CHAPTER 5

On the way back to Billy's home, as luck would have it, they came upon the same bunch of outlaws that had stolen his horse and left him stranded. The farmer tried to talk to the men but they were a hard, cold and ruthless bunch and made a gesture that made the man and the boy believe they were going to once again take the horse as they had done earlier with Billy.

Reaching in his belt and out with the six gun belonging to his dad he fired hitting the leader of the pack and the very one that had taken his horse. Surprised and startled the other men kicked their horses and off they rode leaving the man and the horse behind. The wound was not bad enough to kill the outlaw so they proceeded to town to turn him over to the sheriff as a horse thief and other unlawful deeds.

The sheriff, glad to see the boy as by now the word was out that he had left home. He had always felt sorry for the boy for the Beating he had seen Jed give him and really didn't blame the boy for leaving. I know that you didn't know there was a reward for the man you brought in but he was a wanted outlaw and the reward sure belongs to you Billy because you are the one that brought him in.

Evaluating the situation, the sheriff decided to go with the farmer to deliver the boy back to his parents and to explain what had happened concerning the reward money.

The trip from town seemed, in Billy's mind, to be a long long trip as he had no idea how his dad would react to his activities for the last few months.

Arriving home he was welcomed to the open arm of his mother and the brother and sisters who was glad he had returned. On the other hand Jed was the same man as when Billy had left home. Still angry because the boy had left, taking a horse and gun with him, leaving him to do all the work that the boy was required to do and bring a measure of shame to the family.

He told Billy to get off the place that he didn't need a thief or anybody he couldn't count on around his place.

The other family members were upset and broken, as was his mother, but knowing the kind of man Jed had become knew it would be best for everyone if the boy went on his way.

The sheriff and the farmer tried to talk to Jed telling him that the boy had learned his lesson, with the farmer telling him about what a good farm hand that Billy was and that he had seen him do nothing wrong. Also about how he had saved the day when the outlaws were going to steal the horse and no telling what would have resulted had the young man not took the leader down, besides this boy is a hero for bringing the outlaw in and had earned his reward.

The conversation between the two fell on deaf ears and Jed made no effort to take the boy back in.

Not knowing now what to do he got on the horse and started to ride away when the sheriff stopped him and said,

"We can't let you leave without knowing where you are off to".

At that time the farmer said "I will take you back home with me and you can become just like my son".

After having been rejected again by his dad Billy said

"No thanks you have been kind and thanks for the help you have already given me, but I know if I go with you someday I will bring shame to you and your family too".

The sheriff said "I have an idea, why don't you come back to town with me, be the stable boy and stay in the room at the livery stable. I will see to it you are treated fairly and that you can earn enough to live on and save the reward money to someday buy a place of your own".

Now that sounded like a good idea to Billy and gave him a chance to grow up near his mother and siblings.

"OK he said I'll give it a try and thank you sir".

CHAPTER 6

Arriving back in town he found that everyone was glad to see him and looked upon him as a hero for bringing the leader of the outlaw gang in.

Now the lad was feeling much better about himself and in his mind becoming a valued member of this little western town.

As time passed the job at the livery stable went well while saving the reward money and what little he earned as a stable boy his bank account began to grow.

Now at the age of seventeen he had lived enough to understand what it was to be a man, after all, he had learned about farming ranching, about animals, living on his own, being a hero, saving money and believing he could grow up to be somebody he realized that something was missing.

After having met the prettiest girl in town who was a little younger than he, he realized what was missing. This beautiful girl was named Sarah.

Working hard to build a relationship with the girl was not easy because her father knew all about Billy's past and was very concerned that someday he might be like Jed (his dad) or even do as he had done before and leave town or steal again.

Billy was so excited when he learned that the beautiful daughter of the banker seemed to like him a lot and he would sneak over to her house in late evening and they would go walking for a while. Little time passed and the two found they were very fond of each other but had not yet convinced her dad that it was a good idea causing him to try to stop the relationship any way he could.

This young man had always been head strong and was the kind to be determined to do whatever he wanted to regardless of who tried to stop him. This was no way to earn the favor of the young lady's father but being who he was, he moved forward with his desire for the young woman.

Sarah's dad was always warning her of the danger of falling in love with the wrong man and the possibilities of dealing with a person with a past such as Billy Rime. It was for sure, there were not too many young men in this small settlement to choose from.

Billy had a personality that was a winner and a natural leader at heart so Sarah found it easy to be attracted to him. As the relationship grew stronger so did the opposition from Sarah's father. Of course his interest was only in the future happiness of his only daughter. It was clear to the two young people that Sarah's father would likely never except them being together.

In fact he was overheard telling one of the workers at the bank that he would stop any effort they made for marriage.

The conversation at the bank had now gotten back to Billy so he told Sarah the same and had her to meet him down by the water late that evening. Where the two were together wrapped up in the union of love for the first time.

Later that night Billy went to the saloon, still not old enough to drink liquor in public, told the saloon owner that he let him have a drink when he was only fourteen and he needed to give him another because he was older and really needed to calm his nerves tonight.

"Well, you have grown up quite a bit."

So reluctantly the man gave him a drink and made the mistake of leaving the bottle on the bar which seemed to Billy to be an open door to help himself. True to his character he ended up in a fight and threatened a cowhand with a gun. In no time the word was out and the town folks began to be fearful to be around the boy.

CHAPTER 7

In an effort to stay out of trouble Billy had made friends with the local gambler and was learning the game of cards from one of the best. He encouraged the boy to keep working on the skills he had taught him and said, *"You will never have working a livery stable or as a ranch hand again because you have the gift of being a professional gambler".*

Not, being able to stay away from each other the two young lovers made plans to meet down by the water as they had often done. This being the same place they first could not resist the temptation of their forbidden fruit.

One night Sarah's father followed them and found his only daughter with the boy he had forbidden her to see.

During this encounter Sarah confessed that she was with child and that Billy was the father.

In his anger Sarah's father said

"I will kill you if you ever see my daughter again".

Filled with love for the girl and fear mixed with hate for her father Billy's emotions took charge and with the use of an oak tree root struck the banker and knocked him down. Knowing it was time to leave, but so filled with anger he continued to beat the man leaving him with broken bones and near death. It was Sarah that managed to stop him just before the final blow.

After the fight was over Billy told Sarah that he was going away but that he would be back some day. Stealing a horse from the livery stable, a pair of six guns and rifle by entering the back door of the sheriff's office.

Now having to leave everything he had worked for, his true love and future child behind, he sadly looked over his shoulder, kicked the horse and off he went in search of a place to use his skills in a game of cards in some bigger town where he was not known and the sheriff of his home town could not find him.

CHAPTER 8

Drifting thru the west from one saloon and gambling hall to another building reputation as a high stakes gambler. He found that his skills were well above the average so called gambler and learned that if he bought a couple rounds of drinks for the table he had a much better chance to walk away with a good pot of money.

Of course he had to drink along with the others but he limited is intake to allow him to be the sharpest man in the game.

Everything went his way until one night accused of cheating in a big game a hot headed kid drew on him and the only thing he could do to save himself was to draw and shoot the young kid who, like Billy, should not even have been in this situation. Picking up the winnings stuffing them in his pocket he mounted up and rode on to another town. On the run again, only this time, the word was out that the brother of the young gambler he had shot was out to get him and would be shot on sight.

This was another big change in his trying life. Now with a reputation of a killer Billy felt he must become faster with his gun to stay alive because he knew this would happen again somewhere along the trail.

CHAPTER 9

The days went swiftly as did the months during which time a boy child was born to Sarah. It was her desire to name him Billy after his dad, who she loved and hoped would return as he said to help raise the boy. Sarah's father would have nothing to do with the name Billy so after a while decided to name the boy Seth which was the name of her grandfather who had since passed on.

With the hate still strong for the boy's dad, Sarah's father would have little to do with him and was hard on him as Sarah and the boy was forced to stay with her parents as she had no job means of taking care of herself and the child.

As he grew to an early age of five the boy was assigned chores that w e r e really hard on a young child. With the grit of his dad the boy did his best to get the jobs done without much back talk. Although sometimes he would mutter under his breath comments of unhappiness toward his mother and grandfather.

Seth grew colder toward the family as time passed and was hard to handle at times but folks said.

"Oh that's just the boy in him, he'll be OK."

And a lot of it was true but sometimes it went a little bit farther than that, as people could tell, and Sarah was concerned. Because he had a grandfather and a dad with a strong will and hard headed determination to have things their way.

CHAPTER 10

Back out on the trail Billy was becoming more hardened to the real world that he now found himself in. Upgrading his six guns to a much slicker pair he began to practice hard on his draw and accuracy.

After hours of practice he became as handy with a gun as the average gunfighter. Standing at the bar watching a card game he was approached by an old man who said

"Hey young man, where did you get your hardware?"

Pointing at the six shooter on is hip.

"From a gunsmith in the last town I was in. Looked like a good piece and the action is fine".

The old man looked at him with a strange look and said.

"You think you can use them was good as the last person that owned them, they are not new you know."

Billy caught a strange tone on the old man's voice and followed up with,

"Why did you ask, do you know these guns?"

The reply was rather strong as the old man said *"I sure do and so does a lot of the other people in this region, and most of them are the wrong kind of people to hang around with. If you are going to carry those young man you will have a big set of boots to fill and even then might end up in boot Hill like the last man that carried them."*

Concerned about what the old man said he turned around and headed for the door, but no sooner than he had gone half way across the room he was called out.

An old gunslinger with a reputation of one of the best said *"How many notches on them guns boy."*

"Well they have been slightly used" Billy said.

Finding himself in a rather bad situation. Well now that we have met, let's see if you're good enough to put another one on them. Trying to explain that he was not the original owner of the hand guns and he had not put the notches in the because he had only shot two men, one was an outlaw and the other drew on him in a card game.

The old, hard, gunman was not interested in conversation and called Billy all the names that would make most people mad enough to make the move but Billy resisted. Frustrated the gunman reached for his gun and like a seasoned gun fighter, using his well refined skill, drew and the man fell to the floor.

Not a good feeling Billy thought, to shoot a total stranger down for no reason other than the fact he presented himself as a target for the old man.

Well now the word was out that there was a, fast, gunslinger with several notches on his guns riding thru the area. This was not the way things were to work out in his mind but what could he do now but follow through with the challenge. Moving on to the next saloon big enough to not be noticed for anyone other than a gambler.

The game went well and so did his luck with the lady waiting tables in the place. Planning to hang around for a while he got a room in the hotel and settled in for a hot bath and good meal. Visiting with the lady he had met was his main motivation for staying here for a while. He became known as a rather high classed gambler so naturally the men that felt they were good at the game wanted to get in the game with him.

Dealing with some of the better gamblers that had come to challenge him he was always on the lookout for someone that had recognized him as the gambler who had shot the young man in a game some time ago, after all he knew the boy's brother vowed to shoot him on sight, or someone that had heard of the fast young gunslinger that had taken down the old pro in a town or two back.

Sure enough he was spotted in a saloon and was called to a showdown with one of the well know gunfighters in the area. Not as fast but a much better shot he shot the man down which only enhanced his reputation.

Knowing his welcome had run out in this town checking out of the hotel and moving on was about all that was left to do.

After being on the road, doing all the things he had done still young in age but with the running, hiding, sleeping where ever he ended up, which was mostly out in the rocky, hilly country or in the desert in the heat by day and cold by night had aged his body more than he could believe. He was tired scared and broken down.

Thinking back to when he told the old gunman, that he killed, about shooting an outlaw he remembered the reward money he had received for that deed, he also remembered that he had put the money in the bank back in his home town and had never taken it out. With this thought in mind he couldn't help thinking about Sarah and the child he had never seen and how hard it must be on them to live with the truth of what had caused him to leave town. He had learned along the way from someone the child he had left behind was a boy and they had named him Seth.

There was only one thing to do about this, he knew he couldn't go back and collect the money from the bank, so he went to the telegraph office and sent a telegram to the banker, Sarah's father, to Sarah and to the sheriff telling them about the money he had in the bank and told them to take out enough to pay for the horse he had stolen from the livery stable when he had worked, also for the guns he had taken from the sheriff. The rest was to be taken by Sarah to help raise the boy he had left behind.

By now the stories about Billy's activities had reached home so understanding that he was likely never to return Billy's wishes as to the money in the bank was carried out by the banker, sheriff and Sarah.

Being forced to use his gun more than he wanted to he realized he must practice and become much faster if he was to stay alive. After a time he felt he was the fastest and was confident he would come out standing where ever he went.

CHAPTER 11

Living by the gun and with the desire to have money he was approached by an outlaw who was known to be the top man in a well-known gang.

It was not his desire to become a robber as he felt very good about being able to do well as a gambler but now with the reputation of gun slinging he had to not be seen gambling in the bigger games because someone was sure to recognize him as the fast gun and would try to finish him off and gain the title of the man that beat Billy Rime.

Seemingly the world was closing in on him he felt the need to have partners around him so he agreed to join the gang for a while, thinking someday I will quit and find a place like the little homestead he remembered, maybe even have a family, maybe even finding Sarah and the son he now knew he had.

This gang he was now with was well known for some very ruthless deeds as, bank robbery, stage holdups, outright killing paid for by some people known as prominent rancher, bankers and the like.

These outlaws were known by name and now the name Billy Rime was added to that list. Feared by most gave this gang free range to do whatever the wished to do.

This rough life was after a while getting old and moving on was strongly on his mind.

Whatever he was to do would have to be an effort to leave the wild life he led and do something with a measure of good in it. After another big job he made the move to leave the gang. The boys all tried to talk him out of leaving but his mind was set on a better life so off he rode.

CHAPTER 12

After thinking it over he still couldn't get it out of his head to try something to do that would satisfy the need in his heart to do something worthwhile.

His next move was to hire on a stage line as a shotgun guard which he figured was a respectable job. Traveling a good distance from his now reputation he went to the office of a stage line in an effort to land the job.

When he arrived the boss told him that this was a very dangerous job, and asked him if he was sure he wanted to put his life on the line for the stage company.

"Well don't look at it that way. It would be more like protecting the passengers and shipments against the lawless men who were robbing the stage lines."

The boss told him that the last two guards on this line had been shot mainly because they were not very good shots with a rifle and he felt that a good shooter could make it alright.

"Do you think you are good enough to survive a gun fight. Besides it would have to take someone willing to shoot a man if he needed to."

Billy tried not to show to much confidence as to not bring on conversations of his past but he told the boss that he thought he would be proud of the job he could do.

With that he was hired and was assigned a stage route that went through some of the bad lands known to be hold up territory.

Comfortable with his ability to handle whatever came his way he climbed on the old stage, but unlike most guards he got inside the coach. Taking a seat on the bad side of the trail where the outlaws generally came from as to be ready in the event of a holdup.

The first few runs went off without a hitch and he felt rather good about the job, however, a gold shipment was scheduled on the next run with a large strongbox full of gold. About half way up the trail here they came. Ordering the passenger to get down in the floor Billy opened fire and got two of the gang.

By that time two others had come around from the other side had managed to climb up on top of the stage ordering the driver to stop the stage. He now had figured out what was going on he fired through the top of the stage hitting one of them. The other had the driver at gun point so stopping the stage was the only thing- to do was stop the stage and give up the strong box.

After the outlaws seeing Billy, they realized who he was and had-ridden with him in the past. To save the day he told them that he was going to take the gold by himself but realized he couldn't do that so he was glad to see them and wanted to join the gang.

Knowing his reputation, and all the people he had been involved with they believed him and said *"Come on"*. Off the road with the outlaws and gold.

The gang went straight to their hideout with the heavy strong box of gold. Never having been to this hideout, or with some of this gang he was watched very closely.

Now he knew where they had hidden the gold, and acting as if he knew nothing, he was in time accepted as a good member of the gang.

He told the gang that he had gone to work for the stage coach company in order to learn when and where the gold would be shipped so he could steal it. He also said that he could go back to the stage office and, having a connection there, and tell them the gang had forced him to go with them. That way he could let them know when the exit shipment from the mining co would go out and which stage run it would be on.

They agreed that sounded like a good idea so they let him go and planned a meeting place to pass on the information. He sold the boss on the idea when he got back to the stage office, after all he had shot two of the outlaws.

The next shipment information came out and Billy was assigned to the rum. He figured that he would be found out either by the stage co or the outlaws, in any case would not turn out good he decided to contact the Marshall and tell t hem where the hideout was and that if they knew when the cold run was going to be made the outlaws could be caught red handed.

"What is in it for you?"

The marshal asked to which Billy replied

"Why wouldn't I do this I am guard for the stage lines."

CHAPTER 13

Traveling to a small settlement in New Mexico being many miles from the territory where his reputation was known to be one of the outlaw crowd Billy found the place he would like to start over so he made sure that his appearance was that of a cowboy looking for a job. In no time he was working on a ranch where nobody knew of his past. When asked where he was from his answer was Oh kinda all over with a grin. Just another cowboy that drifted in to town.

Planning for the best but in the back of his mind the thought that he would sometime revisit his past. He sometimes showed his unrest but managed to conform to the new lifestyle.

Becoming an everyday cowboy was a challenge because for so long he was looking over his shoulder for the bad guys or the ones with revenge in their hearts. He made the best of it and was well received by the locals who believed that he was another cowboy drifting from one ranch to another.

The day he was on the lookout for was closer than he expected when a cowboy drifted into town as he had some time ago. He had never seen this cowboy before but he looked like someone he had known from somewhere.

When the boss asked him where he was from Billy felt a chill come across him. He had spent some time there and in fact this is where he had shot the young dude in the card game. Then he realized this had to be the brother who had vowed to shoot him on sight but not looking the same as he did when at the card table the brother did not recognize him.

Knowing that his desire to become unknown cowboy was only a dream he fell back into the realization that his dream of living a normal life could never happen. He had made to a name for himself and most of it was not good. Now it seems it was a sure thing that he would be face to face with the man seeking to revenge his brothers death and would likely end up as to had so often with someone dying. Not knowing how fast this stranger was it could be him that fell this time. Not only that but he would have to stat but he would have to

Strap on his guns again and again he would become known as gun fighter among the friends he had made in this little settlement.

Packing his gear and I not taking time to tell anyone what was going on 1 or collecting his pay, he kept out of sight until late evening mounting up and heading west. He knew how to get his hands on money fast he made straight to the next town with a bank. The bank was not well guarded so Billy had no problem riding away with enough to keep him going for a while.

Back in the business of robbing it was time to round up a couple rough riders, as he had learned it was easier with a hand full of men in a gang. Success in this idea came easy and the rest is a history of serious bank holdups and killings. With wanted posters in every town there was always a bounty hunter or a young cowboy that believed he could beat Billy in a fight and get the reward which by this time was quite handsome. Of course they had little chance in a standoff with Billy the seasoned outlaw.

After many towns and many bank Robbie's he found himself facing a very young boy who said, *"Hey mister someday I want to be famous just like you"*, his mind wondered back to the day he left Sarah who was expecting his son, Seth.

Looking at the boy he figured his son Seth would be about that age and wondering if he had the same desire to be famous as the boy he just met. Knowing this fame had come to him the hard way, he had to do something to set the path of his own son to never do the things he had done, but what could he do.

CHAPTER 14

Meanwhile back in his home town Sarah was bringing up the boy with the help of the banker, Sarah's father. The boy was known to be a lot like his dad and was always asking questions about him. It was hard to tell the boy the truth about his dad for Sarah but then her father had no problem telling the stories of who is dad really was and keeping him informed of the activities he was involved in. Even though everyone was down on Billy the boy somehow admired the outlaw caricature dreaming of someday meeting him and hopefully spending time with him.

Ironically the boy Seth, was working around the stables doing some of the same things his dad had done as a youngster and every day someone would say you sure remind me of your dad. This made the boy even more curious about his dad and more interested in seeing him.

Not old enough to travel alone on horseback Seth got on a west bound stage one day with finding his dad in mind. Of course he didn't get far and was returned home quickly. After Seth pulled this trick Sarah put the word out hoping some way it would get back to Billy and just maybe he could do something to help the situation with the boy before it was too late.

It took some time but he got the story about his boy so now he had to do something but didn't know what to do.

CHAPTER 15

Billy's mind stayed on the boy back home and Sarah being dependent on her father. The more he thought the more determined to right the wrong he had done and set the two he had left up for life on their own.

Could he rob a bank or two and get the money back to them so they would be OK, or was there some other plan that would work better. Knowing that Sarah and Seth were the only heirs of her father and knew he was what was known to be wealthy as the bank owner. He also owned a sizable ranch. Maybe he could have one of the gang go into town as no one would know him and would not suspect him of any wrong doing. While in town he would be able to rob and kill the old man which would set Sarah and Seth for life.

After thinking it over Billy decided that getting Sarah's father out of the way would be a good idea for him but it would be hard on Sarah and the boy not having any family left so his mind went back to work and decided on a better plan. So he set out to follow through with his new idea.

Once again leaving the gang with no word of his plan he set out to his home town arriving in town at high noon on a cool day he had taken measures not to be recognized by wrapping himself in a blanket he had taken from some old Indian. (Normally his sitting in a saddle he was slumped and leaning forward to reduce the risk of being shot by some bounty hunter and it would make it easier to slip off his horse for a fast dismount.)

CHAPTER 16

This time he rode in sitting tall in the saddle. Looking around carefully he spotted a boy on the street and called out to him *"Seth"* he said. The boy reacted to the calling of his name and looked straight at Billy, having no idea it was his dad that he had never meet.

As Seth came closer a lot of memories went through Billy's mind and thoughts of how it would have been if he had stayed in town, married Sarah and raised his son. For a second he had the urge to ride out and go back to his way of life but he knew that his time was limited and that someday he would meet his match and the reward on him would go to some bounty hunter. He had already decided that was not to happen.

As the boy came closer Billy dismounted. With a stranger in town the local people were looking at him trying to figure him out because of the way he was covered with the blanket.

They had no idea this man would ever show his face in this area again, much less ride into town alone.

As he came closer some people could tell it was Billy Mines the outlaw they all knew about and the fear was showing in their eyes. Was it really him, Billy he had been so long ago had changed so much it was hard to recognize him. As he came closer they could tell it was the outlaw, and were clearly concerned that he had returned they had all heard of the things he had done, killing, robbing, thieving etc.

Seeing there was a wanted poster on the door of the saloon of his likeness on it he realized that his plan was coming together. No time to change his mind now. Reaching over he grabbed for the poster and pulled it from the wall.

By this time the boy, Seth, came very close to him. Billy handed the poster to the boy and said.

"Go get the sheriff young man."

As the boy took the poster Billy stood alone until the sheriff came up on the street. With the poster in left hand he realized it was Billy and proceeded to arrest Billy. By raising the shotgun and knowing what the outcome would be. The sheriff fired a fatal shot.

Only one shot came from the forty four that Billy drown and went wildly in the air. Not fired like a gunfighter but like an amateur. Uncannily slow. Seth standing by the sheriff and could hardly believe what had he had seen and that he had been a part in it.

"Well son the reward is yours son." Said the sheriff.

Seth looked puzzled as he looked up at the sheriff and said

"But why did he pick me to call you here sir" to which the sheriff responded.

"BECAUSE THE MAN ON THE GROUND IS YOUR PA."

CHARACTERS

Kenneth Fly as Billy

Finn Carney as Seth (Billy's Son)

Ethan Frame as Sheriff

Patrick Frame as Bystander

Joel Frame as Bystander

GALLERY

THE REWARD

By Kenneth Fly

July 12 2023

www.ingramcontent.com/pod-product-compliance
Lightning Source LLC
LaVergne TN
LVHW041716060526
838201LV00043B/768